LADY HAHN
and her
SEVEN FRIENDS

Yumi Heo

Christy Ottaviano Books
Henry Holt and Company
New York

For Alex

허 보 은

Henry Holt and Company, LLC
Publishers since 1866
175 Fifth Avenue
New York, New York 10010
mackids.com

Library of Congress Cataloging-in-Publication Data
Heo, Yumi.
Lady Hahn and her seven friends / by Yumi Heo. – 1st ed.
p.   cm.
"Christy Ottaviano Books."
Summary: A seamstress banishes her tools from her sewing box when she hears
them boasting, but she discovers that she cannot do her work without them.
ISBN 978-0-8050-4127-9
[1. Sewing–Fiction. 2. Pride and vanity–Fiction.] I. Title.
PZ7.H4117Lad 2012   [E]–dc22   2011005915

First Edition–2012 / Designed by Elynn Cohen
Oil and pencil on 140-pound Fabriano paper were
used to create the illustrations for this book.
Printed in China by South China Printing Company Ltd.,
Dongguan City, Guangdong Province

1 3 5 7 9 10 8 6 4 2

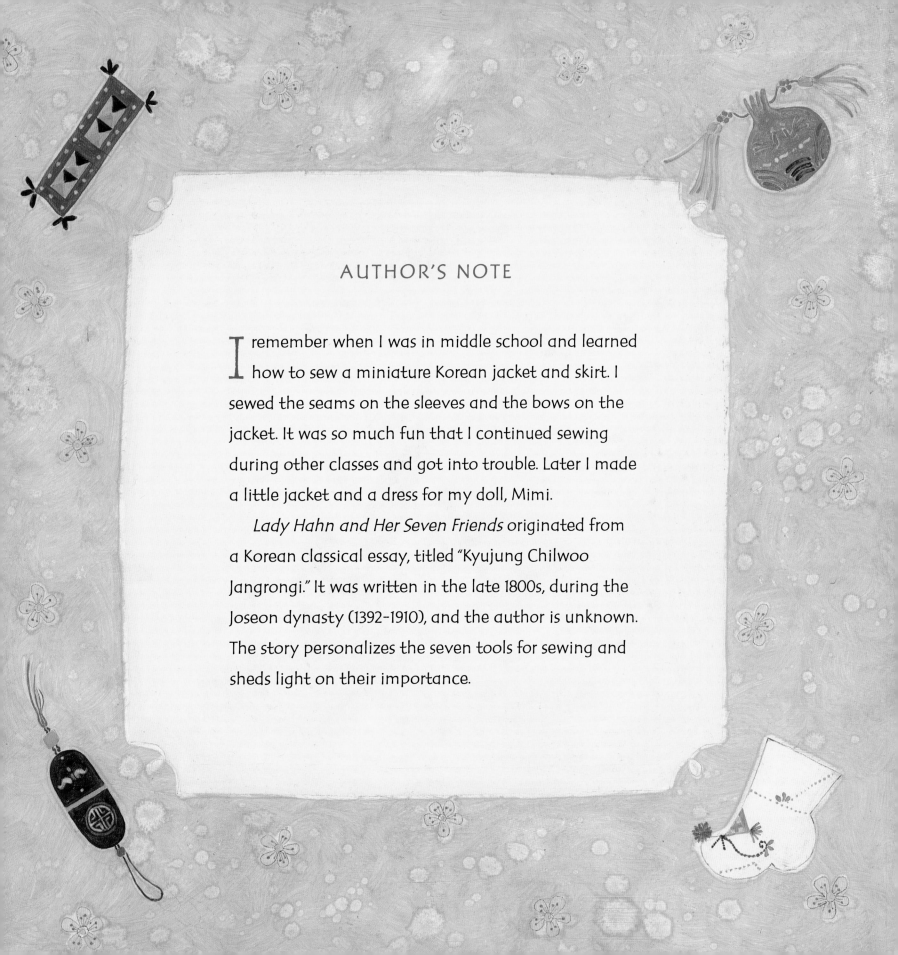

AUTHOR'S NOTE

I remember when I was in middle school and learned how to sew a miniature Korean jacket and skirt. I sewed the seams on the sleeves and the bows on the jacket. It was so much fun that I continued sewing during other classes and got into trouble. Later I made a little jacket and a dress for my doll, Mimi.

Lady Hahn and Her Seven Friends originated from a Korean classical essay, titled "Kyujung Chilwoo Jangrongi." It was written in the late 1800s, during the Joseon dynasty (1392-1910), and the author is unknown. The story personalizes the seven tools for sewing and sheds light on their importance.

Long, long ago when tigers still smoked pipes, there lived Lady Hahn. Lady Hahn's job was to sew shirts and skirts. In her room, she had seven friends: Mrs. Ruler, Newlywed Scissors, Young Bride Needle, Young Bride Red Thread, Old Lady Thimble, Young Lady Flatiron, and Little Miss Iron.

One day, Mrs. Ruler stood up and boasted about her height. "The reason Lady Hahn sews so well is all thanks to me. I tell her just how long and how wide the silk for her shirts should be. I am the most important of all."

Newlywed Scissors walked in quickly and said, "You forgot about me. You talk only about yourself. How good is measuring the silk well if you cannot cut it? I am the most important of all."

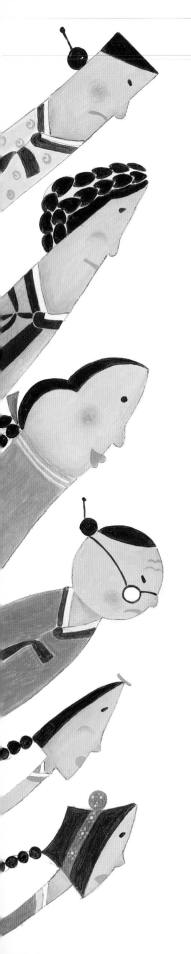

Young Bride Needle

showed off her thin waist and said scornfully, "The shirt cannot be made from just measuring and cutting. Three thousand beads can be a beautiful treasure only after being threaded by a needle. I am the most important of all."

Young Bride Red Thread snorted and exclaimed, "Ho, ho, ho! Poor Needle! It doesn't matter how well you go this way and that way. Without my thread you cannot accomplish anything. I am the most important of all."

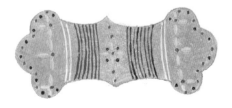

Old Lady Thimble was knocking
on the floor with her back scratcher and shouted,
"Ahem! Who is taking care of Lady Hahn's thumb
day and night? Sewing cannot be done with a
sore finger. I am the most important of all."

Young Lady Flatiron finally blurted out, "All of you boast too much about yourselves. Who flattens all the wrinkles in every corner of the shirt and makes it look good? I am the most important of all."

At last, Little Miss Iron said with blushed cheeks, "What good are flattened shirt corners if there are wrinkles across the shirt? With one press, I make all creases disappear. I am the most important of all."

When Lady Hahn heard the rambling arguments, she grew angry and yelled at her friends. "I cannot believe what I have heard! Without my hands none of you could do your jobs well. I am the most important of all."

Lady Hahn shoveled her seven friends into the sewing box. She turned her back and went to nap.

Startled, the seven friends lost their words.

But soon they cried.

"Lady Hahn forgets all about me after the measuring is done," complained Mrs. Ruler.

"I am thrown on the floor when my legs are dull," said Newlywed Scissors.

"Lady Hahn breaks me in half when I make a tiny mistake," said Young Bride Needle, frowning.

"She balls me up when I get tangled." Young Bride Red Thread sighed.

"I get pricked saving Lady Hahn's thumb and it hurts," said Old Lady Thimble, sobbing.

"Lady Hahn puts me in a hot fire." Young Lady Flatiron teared.

"I am pushed down so hard," said Little Miss Iron, sniffling.

They all decided to leave the sewing box. After climbing out, they scurried behind the lovebird screen.

When Lady Hahn woke up, she returned to her sewing. Then she put her hand in the sewing box to grab her seven friends. None were there. Lady Hahn looked everywhere for them.

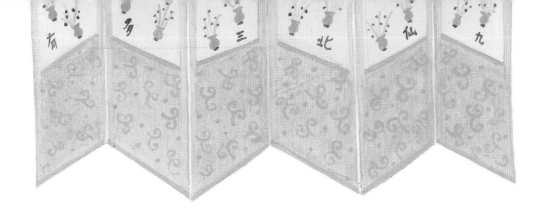

"Mrs. Ruler! Newlywed Scissors! Young Bride Needle!
Young Bride Red Thread! Old Lady Thimble! Young Lady
Flatiron! And Little Miss Iron!" called Lady Hahn.
But her seven friends were gone.

That night, Lady Hahn tried to continue sewing the shirt.

"Oh, no! I cannot tell if the sleeve is long enough. I am not able to cut extra silk from the bottom seam. I am not able to hem the front. My shirt is all wrinkled and my thumb hurts. Please, come back! Please!" begged Lady Hahn.

From behind the screen the seven friends heard Lady Hahn crying. "Poor Lady Hahn! She needs us!" said Old Lady Thimble. They felt sorry about leaving the sewing box and hurried back after Lady Hahn went to bed.

The next day, Lady Hahn was delighted to see her seven friends in the sewing box.

"I am sorry for what I said. I forgot how important all of you are. A shirt cannot be made even if one of you is missing." Lady Hahn and her seven friends smiled at one another.

Ever since then, Lady Hahn and her seven friends sew happily together.